From his home on the other side of the moon,
Father Time summoned eight of his most trusted
storytellers to bring a message of hope to all children.
Their mission was to spread magical tales throughout
the world: tales that remind us that we all belong to one
family, one world; that our hearts speak the same
language, no matter where we live or how different we
look or sound; and that we each have the right to be
loved, to be nurtured, and to reach for a dream.

This is one of their stories.
Listen with your heart and share the magic.

FOR SYLVIE AND
HER UNCLE RICK,
WHOSE CAPACITY
TO LOVE HAS
AWAKENED OUR
HEARTS.

Our thanks to artists Shanna Grotenhuis, Jane Portaluppi, and Mindi Sarko,
as well as Sharon Beckett, Yoshie Brady, Andrea Cascardi, Solveig Chandler, Jun Deguchi,
Akiko Eguchi, Liz Gordon, Tetsuo Ishida, William Levy, Michael Lynton, Masaru Nakamura,
Steve Ouimet, Tomoko Sato, Isamu Senda, Minoru Shibuya, Jan Smith, and Hideaki Suda.

THE RAGGED PEDDLER

Inspired by an Old Middle Eastern Tale

Flavia Weedn & Lisa Weedn Gilbert

Illustrated by Flavia Weedn

Hyperion • New York

Not long ago, at the foot of a mountain, there was a small village in which the people complained and grumbled most all of the time.

They were never satisfied with anything they had
and were always arguing and unhappy. Everyone
who lived in the village worked for a living,
so they each had a home, enough food
to eat, and clothes to wear. But every one
of them thought that his or her
own problems were dreadful
and so much greater
than anyone else's
in the village.

They complained constantly when they
should have been happy and joyful
and thankful for such a good life.

They never noticed that in the spring and
summer the fields at the foot of the mountain
were beautifully green and that bright flowers
grew all around them.

And when the snow covered the mountain in the winter, it glistened dazzling white in the sunshine and glowed a faint rosy pink at sunset. The people never thought how lucky they were to live in a village that was surrounded by such beauty.

One day a stranger
came into town.
He was a peddler who
wore a ragged coat
and an old ragged hat.
He carried a tattered
umbrella, and a big
basket was slung
over one shoulder.

Around his belt,
a rope was wound
many times, and his
boots were patched
and worn.

He walked to the center of the town, then stopped and said, "Your mountain shines like burnished gold, and your rooftops and spires reflect the rosy color of the beautiful sky about you, yet you are unhappy. Come sit beside me, all of you, I have come to sell you happiness."

The people all laughed and called him a fool. "You
not only look like a fool," they said, "you also sound
like one. You bring with you nothing but a rope and
an empty basket. How can that ever give us happiness?"
And they laughed even louder as they continued to
scorn this stranger.

But the peddler just smiled, said nothing, and handed the rope to one of the children. Although doubtful, the people were a bit curious, so they all gathered around to watch.

As the child pulled, the peddler spun 'round and 'round like a top until the rope lay upon the ground in a pile as high as the basket.

Then he threw one end
of the rope to the opposite
side of the street, where it
caught on a tree, and
he looped the other
end around a post near
where he stood.

"My store is now open," the peddler said, "and I am ready for business. So all of you who are unhappy, bring to me your miseries and your discontentments. Place them inside my basket here and I will trade them for happiness."

The peddler watched
the villagers as they
whispered and talked
among themselves.

"He's even a bigger fool than I thought," laughed one of them.

"It must be a trick," whispered another.

Then a voice cried out, "Let's do it and see what happens!"

"What can we lose except our unhappiness?" said another.

So in spite of their disbelief, they put all their complaints into the stranger's basket.

Then the ragged peddler took the basket and lifted it onto the rope, where it balanced itself. Suddenly it began to roll from one end of the rope to the other.

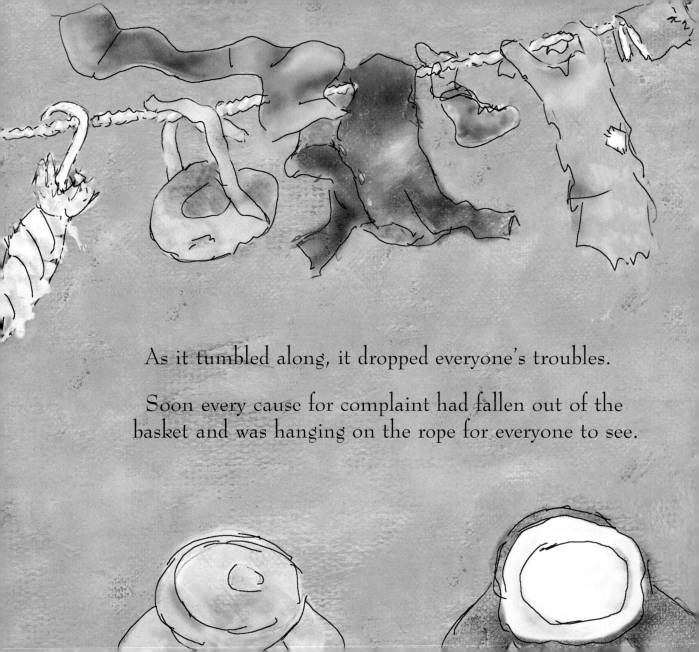

As it tumbled along, it dropped everyone's troubles.

Soon every cause for complaint had fallen out of the basket and was hanging on the rope for everyone to see.

There was the fisherman's

worn-out sweater . . .

the baker's red hair . . .

the tailor's cane . . .

and the flower lady's

tattered shoes.

"Now, good people," the peddler said, "you need only to do one thing. Each of you must line up and take from the rope that which you believe to be the smallest trouble that you see here."

There was a great silence among the people as they each thought about what the ragged peddler had said.

The fisherman looked closely at all the complaints and said to the tailor, "I hated my sweater because it had holes in it, it's faded, and one of the buttons is missing. But now I'd rather have it than anything else. I can find new buttons and patch the holes, and faded just means my sweater is a different color."

Then the baker spoke up. "What would I do with a cane or a worn-out sweater? I've complained about my red hair because it made me look different from anyone else in the town. But I see now that it is the same color as my father's hair. It is a part of who I am, and I should be very proud of it!"

Laughing, the flower lady said to the tailor, "Wouldn't my shoes look funny on any of you? I never thought of it before, but I could polish my shoes and they would be like new. I want to keep them!"

The tailor, looking at his cane, said, "My cane is strong and helps me to walk. Why ever did I complain about it? Actually, I'm quite thankful for it!"

Soon it became clear that each considered their own complaint or trouble to be the smallest one hanging there on the rope.

Quickly they grabbed their own troubles back,
and within a few seconds the line was empty.

"Has each of you taken the smallest trouble?"
asked the peddler.

"Yes!" they cried.

"Then be happy!" he said, and taking his basket and rope, he slowly walked away.

From that moment on, the people of the village never had cause to complain or grumble again, for they had learned a valuable lesson from the wise stranger who had visited their town.

And now this tiny little village, resting so
beautifully at the foot of the mountain, became
a happy and joyful place to live.

Produced in cooperation with Dream Maker Studios AG.
Printed in Singapore.
For information address Hyperion Books for Children,
114 Fifth Avenue, New York, New York 10011.

FIRST EDITION
1 3 5 7 9 10 8 6 4 2

Library of Congress Cataloging-in-Publication Data

Weedn, Flavia.
The ragged peddler: inspired by an old Middle Eastern tale/written by
Flavia Weedn & Lisa Weedn Gilbert; illustrated by Flavia Weedn.
p. cm.—(Dream maker stories)
Summary: In this retelling of a Jewish folktale, a peddler shows a town
of unhappy people that their troubles are not as great as they seem.
ISBN 0-7868-0046-1
[1. Jews—Folklore. 2. Folklore.] I. Gilbert, Lisa Weedn.
II. Title. III. Series: Weedn, Flavia. Dream maker stories.
PZ8.W43Rag 1995
398.2'095602'089924—dc20   94–15053   CIP AC

The artwork for each picture is digitally mastered using acrylic on canvas.
This book is set in 17-point Bernhard Modern.